Dear Parents,

Many years ago, our family discovered a delightful Sleep Fairy who could help us teach our children to stay in bed at night. Since that time, we have shared our discovery with many other parents who overwhelmingly report that the Sleep Fairy really is magical. She will show you a technique that works wonders with children: Simply establish a consistent bedtime routine, read *The Sleep Fairy*, and when your children successfully stay in bed, the Sleep Fairy will leave a surprise while they sleep. With this technique, teaching your children to stay in bed is as easy as sprinkling fairy dust!

With the Sleep Fairy's help, we quickly realized that setting clear expectations for our children made it more likely that they would succeed. We established a few important bedtime rules, and we explained them to our children in a clear and simple way. When our children followed them, the Sleep Fairy would visit during the night and leave a special reward. But it was very, very important for our kids to follow the bedtime rules to get the reward. Not following the rules meant no visit and no reward. And did our kids ever catch on quickly!

It's also very important for you to follow the guidelines. (If you haven't guessed by now, it's up to you to carry out the Sleep Fairy's duties. She can't be everywhere at once, for goodness sake!)

If you forget to reward your cl̶̶̶̶̶ ̶̶̶̶magic will not work. And if a treat is given when the routine isn't followed, your children may never learn the connection between good sleeping habits and getting a reward. Eventually, your children will learn to feel good about staying in bed and falling asleep without whining, crying, or begging. (Believe us, this is the parents' reward.)

Here are just a few tips to help you (and the Sleep Fairy) reward your children. When your children stay in bed and are sleeping peacefully, place a small prize, treat, or charm under their pillows. Choose simple rewards that your children will like, such as a bookmark, sticker, hair ribbon, or small plastic dinosaur. It's not at all necessary to leave expensive items— remember, it's not the gift, but the element of surprise that makes this fun for your children. And be safe; make sure that the reward cannot harm your children in any way. For example, it should not be small enough to swallow, and it should not contain long strings. Keep the prizes simple, safe, and fun. And by all means, praise the dickens out of your children when they follow the bedtime routine!

Teaching your children to stay in bed requires a real commitment from you, your children, and the Sleep Fairy. But the results are worth it.

When you are ready to introduce *The Sleep Fairy* into your family, follow these guidelines:

⭐ When you first begin, read *The Sleep Fairy* every night.

⭐ Once your children have stayed in bed throughout the night and have been rewarded by a visit from the Sleep Fairy for at least two weeks, you will be ready to read the story every other night instead of every night. At this point, tell your children that the Sleep Fairy will visit after two nights of staying in bed.

⭐ After your children have been successful and have enjoyed a visit from the Sleep Fairy every other night, slowly phase out how often you read the story. As time goes on, explain to your children that the Sleep Fairy will become only an occasional visitor.

Eventually, your children will feel comfortable staying in bed without the aid of *The Sleep Fairy* story. Each child is an individual; some may need the Sleep Fairy for a few months, and some may need her magic for a longer period of time. But whether it's a long or a short lesson, you now have discovered a wonderful way to teach your children to stay in bed. (So that all of you can get some rest.)

The Sleep Fairy is a resource for you to adapt to your own family. Feel free to add details to the story that more closely match your own children's bedtime routine. For example, you might include washing faces, setting out tomorrow's clothes, or saying prayers. And you may wish to add other specific instructions you would like your children to follow before the Sleep Fairy arrives, such as, "No talking with your sister after the lights are out" or "Getting up to use the bathroom is okay, but you cannot call out for Mom or Dad." One more thing—we know how hectic bedtime can be, so at times you may wish to read only the poem instead of the entire story. Have fun introducing *The Sleep Fairy* into your family in a way that works for all of you.

Enjoy the benefits of this magical story and technique. And most of all, we hope that you and your children enjoy a peaceful night's sleep.

You might also try our *Behave'n Kids Parent Guide* series for teaching better behavior. See our website for details!

Pleasant Dreams!

Janie and Macy Peterson

www.BehavenKids.com

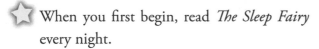

The Sleep Fairy

Janie Peterson
Macy Peterson

BEHAVE'N Kids Press, Inc.
Omaha, Nebraska

Published by Behave'n Kids Press, Inc.
8922 Cuming St.
Omaha, NE 68114
(402) 926-4373
www.BehavenKids.com

First Printing, 2003, hardcover ISBN 978-0-9714405-0-0
Second Printing, 2004, hardcover ISBN 978-0-9714405-0-0
First Printing, 2009, paperback ISBN 978-0-9714405-2-4

Publisher's Cataloging-in-Publication Data
Peterson, Janie
     The Sleep Fairy / Janie Peterson, Macy Peterson;
     Illustrations by Shawn Newlun
     —Omaha, NE : Behaven Kids Press, 2003.

     p. ; cm.

     Audience: ages 2-10.
     Summary: A magical story that will help parents reduce their children's bedtime struggles and nighttime awakenings.

     ISBN 978-0-9714405-2-4
          1. Bedtime—Juvenile fiction. 2. Children—Sleep—Juvenile fiction.
          I. Peterson, Macy. II. Newlun, Shawn

PS3616.E847 S64 2003   2002094458
813.6[E] —dc21   0301

Project coordination by Concierge Marketing, Inc.
Illustrated by Shawn Newlun

10 9 8 7 6 5 4 3

Printed in the United States of America

Dedication

The Sleep Fairy is dedicated to Roger, my husband and best friend.
Your endless support, encouragement and love have made *The Sleep Fairy* possible.

Acknowledgments

I would like to acknowledge the contributions, patience and perseverance of everyone involved in the development of *The Sleep Fairy*. I would like to extend a special thank you to the children (Jimmy, Corbin, Amanda, Kenzie, Madelyn, Jacob, Ellie and Monica) for validating the book's appeal and to their parents for enduring the paperwork to help prove the positive effects of the book. I would like to thank Dr. Raymond Burke and Dr. Brett Kuhn for their patience and expertise in research and sleep disorders. Thanks to Susan Pittelman, Lisa Pelto, Ron Herron, and to my family for editing all aspects of the book. And last, a very warm, loving thanks to my daughters, grandkids, husband, colleagues and family for their support and encouragement.

It was time for bed.

Molly and Katie took their baths.

They brushed their teeth and hair,
wriggled into their pajamas,
sipped their last drinks of water,
and cuddled into their nice, warm beds.

Dad read a bedtime story, and Mom tucked
them in. After kisses and hugs and goodnights
all around, it was time to go to sleep.

Mom and Dad smoothed down the covers,
smiled at the sleepy girls, and tiptoed out of
the quiet room.

Minutes later, Molly peeked around the corner of the stairs. "Mom?" she called, "Mom? I'm thirsty." Mom looked surprised.

"Molly," she said, "you've already had a drink. Go back to bed." Molly trotted back to her warm bed.

Soon Katie appeared. "Dad?" she called. "Dad? Can I have another kiss goodnight?" she asked.

Dad frowned. "Katie," he said, "we have already kissed you from your nose to your toes! Now go back to bed." Katie pouted and stomped back to bed.

But Molly and Katie didn't stay in bed.

A little while later, both girls appeared
at the top of the stairs begging,

"Mom? Dad?
Can you read us another story?"

But Mom and Dad did not budge. They shouted:

"GO BACK

TO BED!"

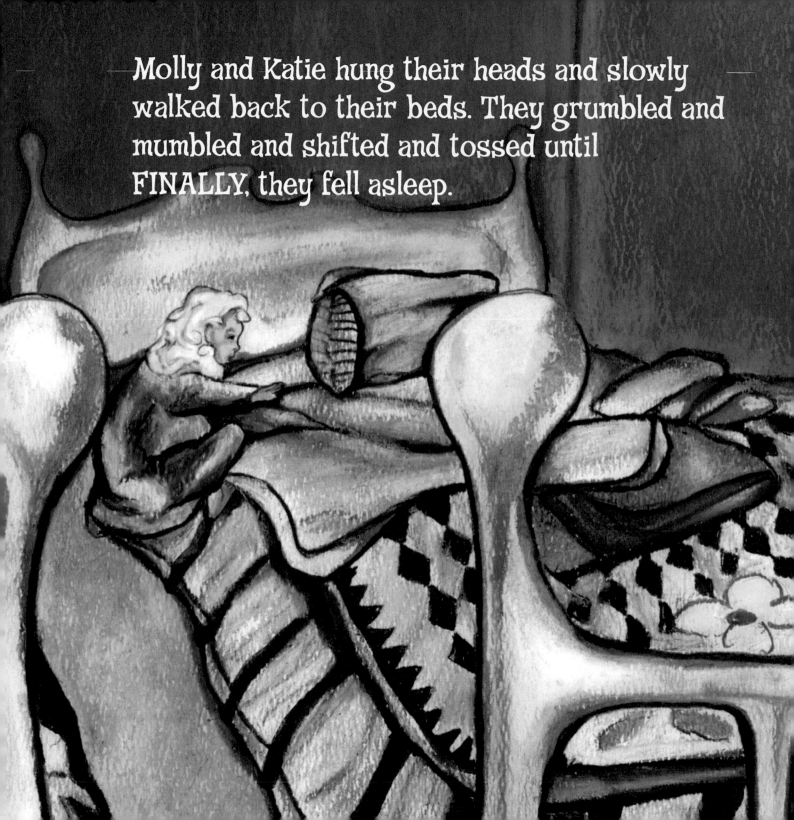

Molly and Katie hung their heads and slowly walked back to their beds. They grumbled and mumbled and shifted and tossed until FINALLY, they fell asleep.

The next night, it was time for bed again.

As always, Molly and Katie took their baths.
They brushed their teeth and hair.
They wriggled back into their pajamas,
sipped their last drinks of water,
and cuddled into their nice, warm beds.

But this night was different.
This night was special.

For on this night,
Mom and Dad read them a very magical story.

Tonight is a special night and you are warm and snug.

You sipped your final drink and you gave us your nightly hug.

I sit here by your bedside and I hold you in my arms,

as I tell you of the Sleep Fairy and all her special charms.

The Fairy's name is Macy; she's beautiful and true.

She wears a magic, sparkling gown and has a gift for you.

She now begins her journey, flying swiftly to and fro.

She watches over children and decides where she will go.

And if you're very still and quiet, and if you stay in bed,

Macy lifts your pillow to place a gift beneath your head.

But she only leaves a present if you stay in bed all night.

So don't yell or cry or leave your bed. Don't pout or whine or fight.

Instead, just snuggle softly in your covers. Shed no tear.

Know that you are safe and loved; the Sleep Fairy is near.

So if you'd like a magic gift, be sure to stay in bed,

and when you wake up in the morning, peek beneath your head.

Now stay in bed all snug and warm and try to fall asleep,

so the Sleep Fairy can come tonight and leave a special treat.

Molly and Katie looked at each other. Their eyes were wide and hopeful. "Do you think the Sleep Fairy will visit us?" whispered Molly. "I hope so," said Katie. "Let's wait quietly and see." Mom and Dad kissed them goodnight. They smoothed down the covers, smiled at the sleepy girls, and tiptoed out of the quiet room.

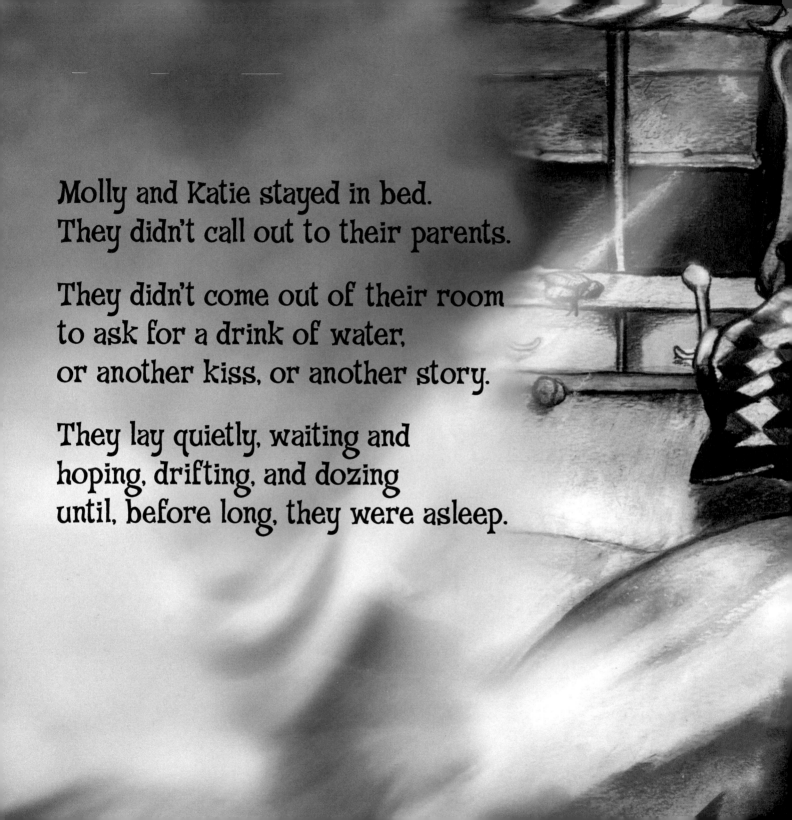

Molly and Katie stayed in bed.
They didn't call out to their parents.

They didn't come out of their room
to ask for a drink of water,
or another kiss, or another story.

They lay quietly, waiting and
hoping, drifting, and dozing
until, before long, they were asleep.

Morning came and the girls awoke.
Molly and Katie quickly looked under
their pillows and cheered,

"THE SLEEP FAIRY
WAS HERE!"

Under each of their pillows was
a special prize.

Molly found a shiny new red ribbon
for her hair, and Katie discovered a
tiny, lovable doll.

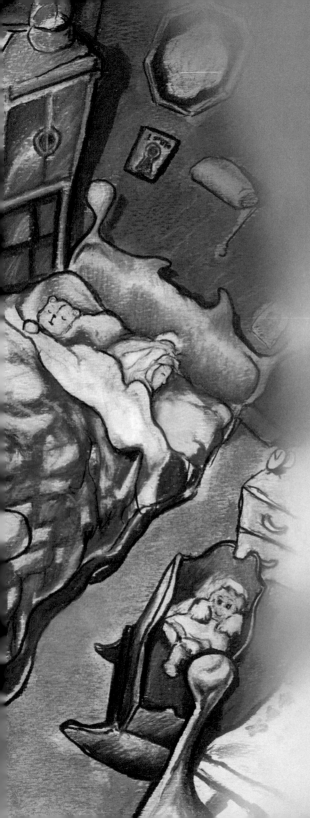

Each night after that, Molly and
Katie asked their parents to read
The Sleep Fairy story.

On the nights they read the
story, stayed in bed,
didn't call out or
ask for a drink of water
or another kiss,
the Sleep Fairy visited
while they were sleeping.

And each morning, under their
pillows, Molly and Katie found
new small presents
the Sleep Fairy had left them
for staying in bed.

So, if you want the Sleep Fairy to come and leave a special present under your pillow. . .

Don't call out or ask for another drink of water.

Don't ask for another kiss or another story.

Rest quietly.
Stay in bed.
Think pleasant thoughts and...

The **Sleep Fairy**

will come to see you tonight.

36157622R00020

Made in the USA
Middletown, DE
25 October 2016